TUMFORD
THE TERRIBLE

Nancy Tillman

FEIWEL AND FRIENDS

NEW YORK

In the wee little village of
Sweet Apple Green,
in the tiniest cottage you've ever seen,
lives a cat causing trouble
within and without…

a cat named Tumford…
Tumford Stoutt.

But love isn't measured in muddy galoshes
or broken tea dishes
or trampled-on squashes.

No, love is a thing that just happens, you see…
like the way I love you
and the way you love me.

And so it goes Georgy and Violet Stoutt
loved their cat Tumford day in and day out.

They fed him with Violet's Twinklefish pie
and they nicknamed him Tummy....

Can you guess why?

But oh dear, and oh my, there was one small pity.
Tumford, it seems, was a most stubborn kitty.
In spite of the manners he often forgot,
he would not say, "I'm sorry."

Oh no, he would not.

Instead, do you know what that Tumford Stoutt did?

Well, I *see* you've guessed it.
That's right.

Tummy hid.

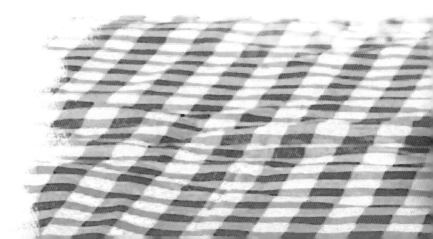

Of all of the things
he thought were the worst…

saying "I'm sorry" most surely came first.

One day, Vi and Georgy both said to each other,

"As Tumford Stoutt's father and Tumford Stoutt's mother,
we could try a plan of a different kind.
Perhaps with a treat, Tummy might change his mind.

In the village today, there'll be a big fair.
It would be grand if we all went there."

"But Tummy," Vi said, "look me straight in the eyes.

If you make a mess, you'll apologize.
You must promise, Tummy, one hundred percent."

"I promise," said Tumford.

And off they all went.

But as Violet was eating and Georgy was pitching,
out of the blue, Tummy's nose started twitching.
Something smelled marvelous over the hedge.

My! He could see it, right there on the ledge.
It wasn't his usual baked Twinklefishes,
but kippers…his favorite of all fishy dishes.

Before they could join in a game of Red Rover,
Tum had forgotten himself and jumped over.

Oh! Then the crash and the squeals and the shouts!
Oh! Then the trouble that met Tumford Stoutt!

Heavens and stars! Of all Sweet Apple Green,
Tum had spilled fish on the Village Fair Queen.

And I'll bet you know just what Tumford Stoutt did.

That's right, you guessed it.

Tumford Stoutt hid.

"Those words are just awful!" he thought. "I can't do it!"
(They'd stick in his throat and he'd choke, he just knew it.)

It wasn't that he was all bad, Tumford Stoutt.
It just was so hard to get those words out!

But then, as he hid, a new thought started growing.
It warmed up his tummy and toes, and kept going.
The thought grew so large that he said it out loud.
"It might feel good if I make the Stoutts proud.
It might make them happy and me happy, too.
Maybe that's why it's the right thing to do!"

I'll bet you've guessed what comes next in the story.
Tumford stepped forward and said he was sorry.
He meant those words too, and what's better than that?
(For nothing is worse than an insincere cat.)

Both the Stoutts cheered, then the crowd
cheered again…
because everyone
felt so wonderful then.

And Tummy? Well, Tummy just sat back and purred
at the wondrous effect of that one little word.

And so, there you go, that's the end of the story
of how Tumford Stoutt finally said he was sorry.

There aren't always cheers when he knocks
over platters,
but he's always loved . . .

and that's all that matters.

To my southern mama, who taught me the importance of good manners.

A FEIWEL AND FRIENDS BOOK
An Imprint of Macmillan

Library of Congress Cataloging-in-Publication Data Available

ISBN: 978-0-312-36840-1

Book design by Nancy Tillman, Rich Deas, and Kathleen Breitenfeld

Feiwel and Friends logo designed by Filomena Tuosto

First Edition: 2011

10 9 8 7 6 5 4

mackids.com

Enormous thanks to my wonderful art director, Rich Deas—N.T.

You are loved.